S0-ACR-794

It Happened to Herbie

By Michaela Friends

Illustrated by Tamara Greeno

Copyright © 1995 Storytellers Ink

All Rights Reserved

No part of the contents of this book may be reproduced or transmitted in any form or by any means, electronic, photocopying, recording, or otherwise, without the written permission of the publisher.

ISBN 1-880812-21-5

8 10 9 7

Published by Storytellers Ink
Seattle, Washington

Printed in the United States of America

To Theodore G.
for his great strength and courage

A mother hedgehog

was searching for food

with Herbie her son

and the rest of her brood.

They used their noses

and listened for sound,

needing very little light

to forage around.

While sniffing and snooping

and scratching along,

their mother stopped still—

she sensed something wrong.

Their spines stood upright!

Not one made a sound.

Was a big, hungry badger

out nosing around?

Their instinct was quick—

each rolled in a ball

with spines sticking out,

protected from all.

Herbie thought he was safe

till he started to roll,

pushed by the badger

down a rather steep knoll.

Herbie tried to be calm.

He was now all alone!

He was hungry and scared

and far from his home.

Was it safe to unroll

from his head to his tail?

He wanted to search

for a bug or a snail.

A storm was now brewing.

Lightning flashed in the sky,

followed by thunder

booming down from up high.

Where was his family?

He wondered in vain.

The scents were all mixed

by the wind and the rain.

He tried to find shelter

as the thunder rolled on—

a place that was safe

to wait until dawn.

An old hollow log

seemed just about right.

Herbie scrambled inside

and slept through the night.

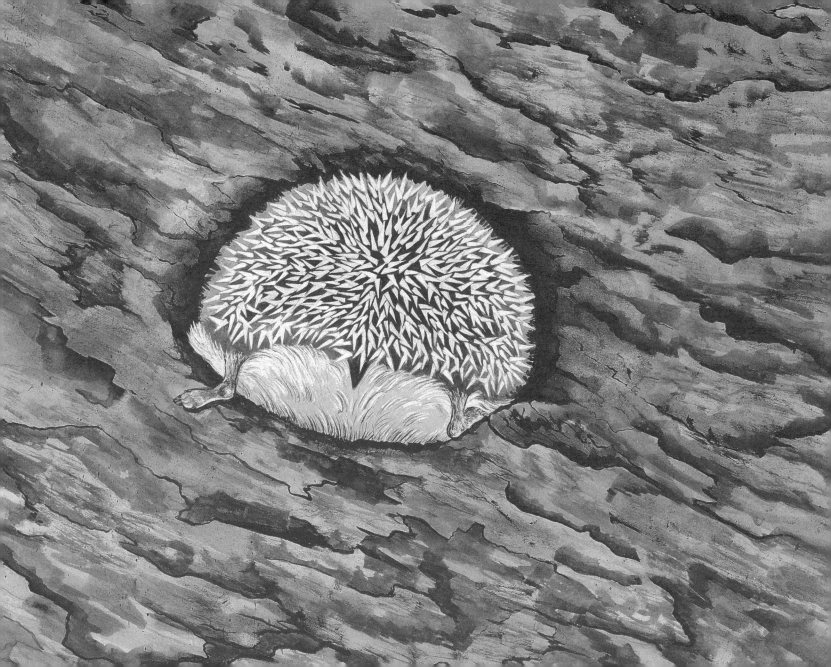

When he finally crawled out

at the first light of day,

he was hoping for help

in finding his way.

Lucky for Herbie

a friend came along.

It was Chickadee Chili

chirping her song.

Herbie knew very well

that sweet melody.

She would sing near his home

from her nest in the tree.

He scurried to follow

as she flew toward her nest,

hoping she'd lead him

to the place he loved best.

As they came near his home

the sky above cleared,

and ahead through the trees

a rainbow appeared.

Herbie's family came out

from the burrow's front door,

and they frolicked and played

all together once more.